This book belongs to:

_____

Dedicated to my first grandson, Mac, and to children everywhere who love nature and wildlife.

Jackson Hole's *Carl* Discovers Wildlife Art

Lynn Estes Friess · John Potter

Mariposa Ranch Press

Carl was always asking questions. "Dad, how tall does sagebrush grow? Why is flax so blue?"

"He's going to be a botanist," his father thought. He gave Carl books on plants and trees.

"Mom, why do rabbits hop? How high can a crow fly?"

"Maybe he'll be a wildlife biologist," his mother thought.
She gave Carl books on animals and birds.

So Carl could find answers to his questions, Carl read

. . . early in the morning,

WHEN GRIZZLIES AND CHIPMUNKS MEET!

. . . before lunchtime to his little sister, Suzy,

. . . when he was supposed to be taking a nap,

. . . outside on his favorite log,

. . . during his long, long bubble bath,

. . . and to his father before bedtime.

Carl loved learning from books.

One day, Carl had just finished reading his favorite book, "Chipmunk Adventures" to his best friends, Marnie Marmot and Willie Mouse when. . .

they heard strange noises and
men's voices over the hill. They
peered through the tall grasses
to see what was happening.

A large truck with a noisy crane squeaked and groaned as it swung about moving and lifting.

Men were yelling to the crane operator. They were guiding elk to be placed on huge rocks.

At dinner, Carl told what he had seen.

"Those statues show the way to the National Museum of Wildlife Art up the hill," said his father.

"What's a museum? Can I go see it? What's inside?"

Carl had so many questions. His father promised to take Carl there as soon as he could.

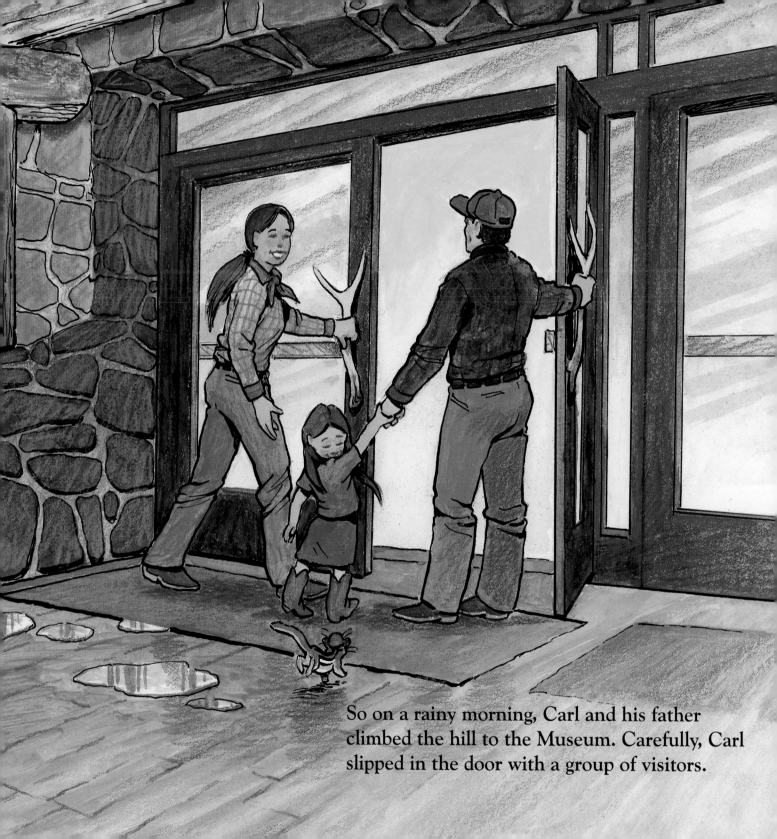

So on a rainy morning, Carl and his father climbed the hill to the Museum. Carefully, Carl slipped in the door with a group of visitors.

He joined a tour led by a man wearing a badge on his vest. He was talking about wildlife art.

After the tour was over, Carl went back to every Gallery. His favorite painting was "Black Bear" by Carl Rungius.

"What a great painter Rungius was and we even share our first name!" exclaimed Carl with delight.

As Carl looked at the easel and paintbox used by Rungius, he KNEW what he wanted to be.

So every night, Carl returned to the Museum Library to study, write notes, and find all the answers to his questions.

Bob, the Security Man, was making his rounds one night and spied Carl taking notes by candlelight.

"Hmmm, no fire allowed in the Museum," he thought. "I'll leave the lights on for the little fellow."

Each day, Carl quietly followed a guide on a tour so he could learn more. There was Walter and Whittredge, Bateman and Barye.

My friends will enjoy all the art here," thought Carl.

"But first I must pass the Guide Test."

So he studied at home every morning. . . .

. . . and at the Museum in the JKM Gallery every afternoon. . .

. . . and at the Museum Library every evening.

One stormy night as lightning flashed and thunder shook the Museum's windows, Carl took the difficult Guide Test.

Next morning, the Head Guide found the test on her desk. Every answer was correct. On the bottom it was signed "CARL!"

"Who is this?" the Head Guide asked Bob, the Security Man.

"Why, that must be the little fellow who's been studying at night in the Library," answered Bob.

"He's passed the Guide Test. Could you please give him this? He's earned it,' said the Head Guide.

"I'd be happy to," Bob replied.

That evening on the Library table Carl found
a surprise that pleased him very much.

So next time you visit the National Museum of Wildlife Art, you just may see. . . .

. . . a small group of animals learning about the oldest art form in the world. . . . wildlife art. . .

. . . led by a small, famous guide, wearing a vest
and his very own badge. . .

Carl!

CARL
Text copyright © 2010 by Lynn Estes Friess
Mariposa Ranch Press
Illustrations copyright © 2010 by National Museum of
Wildlife Art, Jackson Hole, WY

ISBN 978-1-4507-3120-1

Mariposa Ranch Press
P.O. Box 9790
Jackson, Wyoming 83002
(307)- 733-2647
www.mariposaranchpress.com

ILLUSTRATED BY John Potter
WRITTEN BY Lynn Estes Friess
DESIGNED BY Carole Thickstun, www.ormsbythickstun.com
PRINTED RESPONSIBLY BY Paragon Press, Salt Lake City, UT
This publication was printed using Ecotech vegetable based inks
on Opus Matte recycled paper manufactured by Sappi Fine Paper
North America. 100% of the electricity used to manufacture
Opus Matte is Green-e® certified renewable energy. The fiber in
this paper was sourced from well managed forests and contains
10% post consumer waste.

Library of Congress Cataloging pending

NATIONAL MUSEUM
of WILDLIFE ART

Proceeds from this book go to help sponsor programs for
children, adults, exhibits, and to provide operating support
for the National Museum of Wildlife Art, Jackson, Wyoming.
Visit their site at www.wildlifeart.org.